It's Time to Wake Up!

by **Jenny Jinks** and **Tomislav Zlatic**

W
FRANKLIN WATTS
LONDON•SYDNEY

Down on the farm, everyone had
a job to do.
Hen's job was to lay eggs.
Cow's job was to eat grass and
Donkey's job was to pull the cart.

But Cluck thought his job was the most important one of all.
"I have to wake you all up so you can get your jobs done," he crowed.

But Cluck was not very good at
his job.

"When do I wake you up?"
he asked the animals.

"When it is morning," said Hen.

"When the sun comes up," said Cow.

"When I have had a nice,
long sleep," said Donkey.

That night the animals went to sleep,

but Cluck stayed awake.

He wanted to do his job right.

He waited and waited.

Was it morning yet?

"Cock-a-doodle ..." said Cluck.

"Not yet," said Hen.

"Now go to sleep."

But Cluck stayed awake.

He waited for the sun

to come up.

Then he saw a light in the sky.

"Cock-a-doodle ..." said Cluck.

"Not yet," said Cow.

"That's the moon, not the sun.

Now go to sleep."

But Cluck stayed awake.

He waited for Donkey to have

a nice, long sleep.

Then he heard Donkey in the barn.

"Cock-a-doodle ..." said Cluck.

"Not yet," said Donkey.

"I was just snoring."

Cluck was sad.

How would he know when it was

time to wake everyone up?

The sun came up.

But all the animals were still asleep.

Suddenly, Hen woke up. "Wake up!

Wake up!" she said in a flap.

Cow and Donkey woke up.

It was late.

"Why didn't we wake up?" said Hen.

"Where is Cluck?"

Cluck was leaving the farm.

"I am not good at my job,"
said Cluck sadly.

"Wait," the animals said. "We have
something that will help you."
They gave Cluck a box.

Cluck opened the box and smiled.

It was the perfect present.

That night Cluck went straight

to sleep.

Down on the farm, the sun came up.

All the animals were asleep,

when suddenly ...

BRRRRRRRRRRIIIIIIIIIIIING!

"Cock-a-doodle-doooo!"

Cluck shouted. "It's time to get up!"

Story order

Look at these 5 pictures and captions.
Put the pictures in the right order
to retell the story.

1

Cluck is sad.

2

Cluck crows and wakes up Hen.

3

Cluck uses his new alarm clock.

4

Cluck says his job is the most important.

5

Cluck tries to leave the farm.

21

Independent Reading

This series is designed to provide an opportunity for your child to read on their own. These notes are written for you to help your child choose a book and to read it independently.

In school, your child's teacher will often be using reading books which have been banded to support the process of learning to read. Use the book band colour your child is reading in school to help you make a good choice. *It's Time to Wake Up!* is a good choice for children reading at Orange Band in their classroom to read independently.

The aim of independent reading is to read this book with ease, so that your child enjoys the story and relates it to their own experiences.

About the book

Cluck the cockerel knows his job is important, but he just can't figure out when to wake up the other animals! Cluck needs help and his friends know just what to do.

Before reading

Help your child to learn how to make good choices by asking: "Why did you choose this book? Why do you think you will enjoy it?" Look at the cover together and ask: "What do you think the story will be about?" Ask your child to think of what they already know about the story context. Then ask your child to read the title aloud. Establish that in this book they will learn about a cockerel's job on a farm. Ask: "What do you know about cockerels? What sound do they make?"

Remind your child that they can sound out the letters to make a word if they get stuck.

Decide together whether your child will read the story independently or read it aloud to you.

During reading

Remind your child of what they know and what they can do independently. If reading aloud, support your child if they hesitate or ask for help by telling the word. If reading to themselves, remind your child that they can come and ask for your help if stuck.

After reading

Support comprehension by asking your child to tell you about the story. Use the story order puzzle to encourage your child to retell the story in the right sequence, in their own words. The correct sequence can be found at the bottom of the next page.

Help your child think about the messages in the book that go beyond the story and ask: "How did the other animals show Cluck kindness instead of anger?"

Give your child a chance to respond to the story: "Did you have a favourite part? Did you think Cluck would ever get it right? Why/why not?"

Extending learning

Help your child understand the story structure by using the same sentence patterning and adding different elements. "Let's make up a new story about farm animals. Which animal is your story about? What is its job on the farm? How can the other animals help?"

In the classroom, your child's teacher may be teaching how to read words with contractions. There are many examples in this book that you could look at with your child, for example: *it's, don't, that's, didn't.* Find these together and point out how the apostrophe indicates a missing letter.

Franklin Watts
First published in Great Britain in 2020
by The Watts Publishing Group

Series Editors: Jackie Hamley, Melanie Palmer and Grace Glendinning
Series Advisors: Dr Sue Bodman and Glen Franklin
Series Designer: Peter Scoulding

A CIP catalogue record for this book is
available from the British Library.

ISBN 978 1 4451 6872 2 (hbk)
ISBN 978 1 4451 6874 6 (pbk)
ISBN 978 1 4451 6873 9 (library ebook)

Printed in China

Franklin Watts
An imprint of
Hachette Children's Group
Part of The Watts Publishing Group
Carmelite House
50 Victoria Embankment
London EC4Y 0DZ

An Hachette UK Company
www.hachette.co.uk

www.franklinwatts.co.uk

FSC
www.fsc.org
MIX
Paper from
responsible sources
FSC® C104740

Answer to Story order: 4, 2, 1, 5, 3